ATONEMENT

ATONEMENT

Ian Rankin

SHORTLIST

First published in 2005 by
Orion
This Large Print edition published
2012 by AudioGO Ltd
by arrangement with
The Orion Publishing Group

ISBN 978 1 4458 4502 9

British Library Cataloguing in Publication Data available

Printed and bound in Great Britain by
MPG Books Group Limited

'They're dropping like flies.'

The man collapsed into another fit of coughing, doubling over in the tattered armchair. Rebus looked around him, but no one in the large, overheated room was paying the slightest attention. Some were watching a daytime nature programme, others dozing or staring out of the window. It was a large sash window—three windows actually, forming a bay. The paintwork looked new. Rebus thought he could smell fresh paint, its aroma not quite exhausted. There were other smells, too: the remains of a fish lunch; talcum powder and perfume; perished rubber. The redecorating did not stretch as far as the cornices and ceiling. The cornicing was elaborate, the design almost Celtic. The ceiling was pale green, a few veined cracks radiating from the

1

central light fitting.

At one time, this would have been a fine private home, enjoyed by a bank manager and his growing family. Edinburgh had no shortage of these detached Victorian mansions. Some had been divided into flats, of course. Others were business HQs, or owned by large institutions and charities. Renshaw House, however, had become a care home for the elderly, which meant that the man in the armchair must be elderly. His name was Ken Flatley. When Rebus had first joined the police, Flatley had been a mentor of sorts. Not that the word 'mentor' would ever have been used between them: Rebus was a detective, Ken Flatley the uniform who manned the police station's front desk. All the same, the older man had looked at the younger and understood—understood that tips and hints would be appreciated.

This had been in the early 1970s, the era of boot boys and pub rock:

Rod Stewart in his tartan scarf, and Elton John telling teenagers that it was all right to fight on a Saturday night. One such altercation had put Ken Flatley behind the desk: suedeheads clashing after a football derby, Flatley between them quickly becoming their shared target, leaving him with a limp. He used a walking frame these days His thick brown hair had never gone grey, so that strangers sometimes mistook it for a wig. The face below the low fringe was creased but resolute. Take away the walking frame, Rebus reckoned, and his friend would seem younger than himself.

They had lost touch for a number of years, reunited briefly at the funeral of Flatley's wife Irma. But when Rebus had learned Flatley had sold the bungalow in Prestonfield and moved to a nursing home, he'd arranged to visit. That first meeting had not started well, Ken asserting that he needed no pity.

3

'I'm not here for that,' Rebus had told him.

'What then?'

'Maybe I'm just on the lookout,' Rebus had replied, scanning the room. Flatley had caught his meaning and laughed.

'Aye, not too long till you'll be joining me.'

It was a thought Rebus had been pushing away ever since. After all, he was in his late fifties, maybe only fifteen years younger than Flatley. And he lived alone. If anything happened . . . if his faculties started to fail or went into reverse . . . He had no family nearby, and though he would try to cope, try to do everything for himself, there was always the possibility that he would not succeed. When he had first married and moved into the tenement flat where he still lived, there'd been a man on the top floor who'd lived alone. Rebus had always been slightly wary of this man, especially when his daughter Sammy had been young; hadn't even bothered to attend the neighbour's funeral. And yet now . . . now there were students and young couples in his tenement, and he had become the oldest inhabitant.

'Dropping like flies,' Flatley repeated, clutching the arms of the chair. It was his own chair, one of the few possessions he'd been allowed to bring with him from home. Much of the rest had been disposed of at auction, a daughter in Bristol taking only a few mementoes—photograph albums and some bone china. Asked if he had thought of going to stay nearer his daughter, Flatley had shaken his head vigorously.

'Got her own life now,' he'd insisted.

Rebus watched him as he wiped the back of one tremulous hand across his mouth. 'How do you mean?' he asked.

His friend leaned forward, inviting

Rebus to do the same, until their heads were inches apart.

'Faces in here,' Flatley muttered, 'they don't last long.'

Rebus nodded as if he understood, but Flatley gave him the same hard gaze he'd given the young detective whenever Rebus had made some tyro's error.

'I don't mean they just get old and peg it.' He nodded towards an empty chair by the fireplace. 'Mrs Edwards used to sit there. Sprightly, she was, when she came in here. Family said she couldn't cope—what they meant was, *they* couldn't cope. So in she comes and lights the place up . . . until last week. Ambulance came for her, and three days later they tell us she's dead.'

'Ken . . .'

'She's not the only one, John.' Flatley's voice was insistent, knowing the objection Rebus had been about to make. 'Dot Parker took ill one day, died the next. Same with

Manny Lehrer.'

'You're saying they're being bumped off, one by one?'

'It's no joke, John.'

Rebus's smile faded. 'No, I'm sure it's not. So what are we talking about here?'

'I'm not sure . . . There was something in the paper recently about staff in care homes letting people die.'

'Benign neglect?'

'I don't think "benign" enters into it.'

'Are you saying they don't feed you?'

'Oh, they feed us all right . . . after a fashion.'

'What then?'

'You hear about it all the time, don't you? Nurses who're secretly poisoning their patients.'

'Ken . . .' The tone of warning had returned to Rebus's voice. Flatley just stared at him and Rebus sighed, sitting back in his chair. 'What is it you want me to do?'

'I just thought someone should . . .' The words died away. 'You know, when someone dies unexpectedly, even if they're old, there's an autopsy.'

'What if it's not unexpected, though? They've been ill or frail . . . a pathologist is going to find what he expects to find. He's not going to be as thorough as with a corpse with a knife in its back.'

Rebus held his hands up, palms towards his tormentor. He glanced around him, but no one seemed to have heard the outburst. 'If it will help put your mind at rest,' he said, 'let me see what I can do.'

Some of the tension left Flatley's face. He shifted his gaze floorwards. 'Why do you keep coming here, John?'

'Maybe I'm a fan of conspiracy theories.'

'I'm serious.' Flatley fixed him with a stare. 'I mean, it's good to get a visitor now and then . . . I just don't see what you get out of it.'

'Could be I've got a guilty conscience, Ken. All those years I never kept in touch.'

'We have to share the dock then— I'm as guilty as you are.'

Rebus patted his friend's leg. 'Let me do some digging, see if someone really is doing a bit of drastic bed-clearing.' Rebus got to his feet. 'And if I don't find anything, will your mind be at rest?'

'My mind gets too much bloody rest these days,' Flatley snorted.

Rebus nodded slowly: maybe that's the trouble, he thought to himself . . .

*   *   *

'What exactly is it we're being accused of, Inspector?'

Donald Morrison sat back in his black-leather office chair. Rebus was seated at the other side of the desk. Diplomacy had never been his strong point, but all the same, he felt he'd presented the case fairly. Morrison, however, the owner of Renshaw House, was riled. Rebus could tell this because of the way the blood had risen to the man's cheeks.

'As I said, sir, I'm not here in any official capacity . . .'

'But you *are* a police officer?' Morrison waited for Rebus to nod agreement. 'And you're here to visit someone who was also a policeman.' He forced the beginnings of a smile. 'It seems Mr Flatley is finding it hard to give up his old job.'

Morrison rose from his chair and turned to face the window—a replica of the one in the communal sitting room. He clasped his hands behind his back and stared out at the expanse of mown lawn, broken only by a sundial at its centre. There were benches around its periphery, shaded by mature trees. He was broad-shouldered, had probably played rugby in his younger days.

His hair was greying at the ears and temples, thinning on top. There were horizontal creases above the vents of his suit jacket.

'He's free to leave, you know,' Morrison said, patting one hand against the other. 'Our waiting list is substantial.'

'Of people wanting to leave?'

Morrison turned back to Rebus, tried out another smile on him. 'Wanting to get in, Inspector. Time was, there were plenty of care homes, but not any more. So if Mr Flatley really isn't happy here . . . '

'Nobody's saying he's unhappy. He's just worried.'

'Of course he is.' Morrison pulled out his chair and sat down again. 'He's surrounded by people who are not exactly in the first flush of youth. I'm afraid it's part and parcel of the way of things, Inspector. People don't come here to get younger and flourish—I only wish that were the case.' He gave a slight shrug. 'Mrs

11

Edwards and Mrs Parker . . . Mr Lehrer . . . they were in their eighties, and hardly in the most robust health to begin with.'

'Ken's description of Mrs Edwards was "sprightly".'

Morrison pondered this. 'He saw what he wanted to see.'

'You're saying he fancied her?'

'Age doesn't always blinker the heart.'

'And that's why her death has hit him so hard?'

Morrison gave another shrug. 'Do you think you can put Mr Flatley's mind at rest, Inspector?'

'I can try.'

Morrison bowed his head a little, satisfied at this outcome. 'Mortality is sometimes a difficult concept even for the elderly.'

'I don't think it's the concept that's bothering Ken.'

'You're right, of course.' Morrison had risen, indicating that the meeting was at its end. 'It may not help that he doesn't get many visitors.'

'His daughter lives in England.'

'He must have friends . . . ex-colleagues like yourself?'

'I'm not sure he wants them to see him in a care home.'

Morrison chose not to see this as a further slight. Instead he nodded slowly. 'Self-reliance . . . it's something we see a lot of: people too proud to ask for help, even when it's needed.' He held out his hand for Rebus to shake. Rebus took it.

'Just out of curiosity,' he asked, 'what did they die of?' Morrison's face darkened a little, the blood threatening to return to his cheeks. 'Old age, Inspector, nothing more than that.'

'Ken seemed to think they were taken to hospital.'

'Yes?'

'So they all died in hospital?'

'That's right. When a patron weakens dangerously, we're duty-bound to seek medical attention for them.'

'And I'm sure you do so conscientiously.'

'We'd be closed down otherwise.' Morrison reached out to open the door. 'I wish I could feel that I've allayed your concerns, Inspector.'

'I don't have any concerns, Mr Morrison. Thanks for your time.' Rebus was on the other side of the threshold when he stopped and turned. 'I parked my car next to a silver Merc. Is it yours, by any chance?'

'It's mine.' Morrison seemed to be waiting for something more, but Rebus just nodded thoughtfully. 'Nice motor,' he said, turning to leave.

*   *   *

Flatley was waiting for him at the main door. It stood open, letting some much-needed air into the place. Flatley was leaning heavily

14

against his walking frame, but straightened up when he saw Rebus.

'Keeping tabs on me, Ken?' Rebus asked.

'Just contemplating a nice long stroll.'

'Anywhere in mind?'

'Nearest pub's in Marchmont.'

'That's a good half-mile. Maybe I'll join you.'

Flatley's mouth twitched. He looked down at the metal frame against which he leaned. 'Maybe another time, eh? Did you get any joy from the commandant?'

'You're not a fan?'

Flatley wrinkled his nose. 'He's in it for the money, same as the rest of them.'

'I think there's probably better money out there somewhere, Ken.'

'Maybe so, but something tells me he's not giving himself the same minimum wage the rest of the staff have to swallow.'

'Steady, Ken, you're choking the

life out of that thing.'

Flatley followed Rebus's gaze to the frame's rubber hand-grips, then smiled and relaxed his knuckles a little. 'Did you ask him about the body count?'

'I did.'

'Mention my name at all?'

'Hard not to.'

'So that's me on half-rations.'

'No hardship—you don't like the food anyway. I'll bring you a couple of pies next time I visit.'

There was silence between them, punctuated only by the sounds of the TV set in the room opposite.

'You think I'm turning gaga, John?' Flatley's eyes bored into Rebus's.

'No.'

'Maybe I am at that.'

'Maybe you could leave here . . . try making do with a home help.'

'My home's not there any more, John.'

'Then you've got to make the best

of it.' Rebus hated himself for saying the words. They sounded hollow, clichéd. *Make do . . . mustn't grumble . . . He* felt his old mentor deserved more.

There was sudden movement behind them. An elderly man, stick-thin and with a pale, skeletal face, was shambling in their direction, eyes wide at the sight of the open door.

'Oh Christ, it's—' The rest of the sentence went unfinished as Ken Flatley was barged aside by the old man. He stumbled into the wall, dislodging a framed painting. The frame fell apart as it hit the parquet floor, Flatley sliding down after it. A care assistant's head appeared around a doorway.

'Mr Waters!' she called. But by this time, Mr Waters was through the door. Rebus, crouching to help Ken Flatley back to his feet, saw the man waddle down the wheelchair ramp outside the entrance to Renshaw House.

'Mr Waters!' the woman called again. She was striding down the hall now, drying her hands on the front of her sky-blue uniform. Flatley was nodding that he was all right. Rebus made sure his friend had a good grip on his walking-frame, then turned his attention to the fleeing man. Waters was wearing neither shoes nor socks. His upper body was covered only by a white cotton vest, accentuating his thinness His trousers had slipped down far enough to reveal that he was wearing some sort of incontinence pad beneath.

'Need a hand?' Rebus asked the assistant as she passed him. 'I'll manage,' she muttered.

'She won't,' Ken Flatley said, jerking his head to let Rebus know he should follow her. Waters' gait was that of a walker in the Olympics. He seemed to take what weight he had on the balls of his feet, and his arms were pumping, elbows jutting out to either side. He was heading in a straight line across the lawn, towards an eight-foot stone wall. There was dew on the grass, and the care worker's rubber soles went from under her. There was a banana-skin inevitability to her slow, graceless fall. She snatched at a wrenched ankle and let out a roar which brought Mr Waters to a halt. He turned, arms dropping to his sides. Rebus leaned down to help the woman up.

'Any damage?' he asked her.

'Just twisted it.'

An arm around her waist, he brought her to her feet. Mr Waters was standing directly in front of them.

'I can't remember,' he said, voice high-pitched, false teeth missing.

'Remember what?' the woman asked angrily.

'Where the body's buried.'

'Not that again.' She gave a loud hiss. 'There's nobody dead, Mr Waters,' she told him, as if explaining something to a stubborn child.

'She buried the body. I'm not what you think I am.'

'We know who you are, Mr Waters. Your name's Lionel.' She turned to Rebus and rolled her eyes. His fingers were around the bare flesh of her arm. She eased away from him slightly, and he let her go.

'My treasure's all gone . . . The fishing-boat . . . the castle . . . all gone.'

'That's right, Mr Waters, all gone.' She was talking to the man but her eyes were on Rebus, and she was shaking her head slowly, to let him know this was a regular exchange. 'Now let's get you back to the house.'

'I need to see Colin, to tell him I'm sorry. You believe me, don't you?'

'Of course I do.'

But Waters wasn't looking at her. Rebus was his focus. The old man's eyes narrowed, as if trying to place the face. 'Nobody believes me,' he stated.

'You're a bloody nutcase, Waters!' The voice was Ken Flatley's. He was standing in the doorway, while a carer started tidying up the picture frame. 'About time they sectioned you again!' A hand patted Flatley's shoulder, and he turned towards his comforter: Donald Morrison.

*   *   *

Rebus insisted on accompanying the care assistant back to Lionel Waters' bedroom. As she gave the old man a blue tablet and a glass of water, Rebus looked around. The room was bare. He got the feeling all the furnishings belonged to Renshaw House itself. Waters was seated on a chair by his bedside. A tattered magazine was lying open on the bed, showing a half-finished word puzzle.

'What's your name?' Rebus asked the assistant.

'Annie.'

'Sure that ankle's okay?'

'I'll manage.' She was tucking a tartan travel rug around Waters' legs.

'I'd say you've probably got a good case for a day or two on the sick.'

'Maybe so.'

'But you'll manage?'

She turned to him. Her eyes were a deep hazel. 'It's tough enough working here; one goes sick, that just makes it tougher.'

'You're short-staffed?'

'Lousy wages for back-breaking work . . . what do you think?'

'I think I couldn't do it.' His eyes shifted over the walls. 'He didn't bring much with him, did he?'

Annie turned her attention to Waters. He was mumbling, but his eyes had gone glassy, the lids drooping. 'Poor sod was in a mental institution before this. Locked away since his twenties. Never really right in the head, according to the family. Eventually they couldn't cope. He was aggressive, you see.'

'And he killed someone called Colin?'

She smiled at the mistake. 'Colin's his brother. Colin Waters?' Her eyes were on Rebus's again.

'The car dealer?'

'Biggest on the east coast—isn't that what the advert says?'

Rebus nodded slowly. 'He comes from a rich family then. They're paying for this place?'

'I suppose so.' Waters' eyes had closed now. Annie motioned with her head for Rebus to leave. Out in the corridor, she left the door ajar a few inches. The unconscious figure of Lionel Waters could be seen through the gap.

'Why did they let him out of the other place?' *The other place*— because Rebus didn't know what the current term was for a nut-house, a loony-bin, an asylum.

'Said he no longer posed a threat. If you ask me, it's been a long time since he did. All he wants to do is run away.'

'To see his treasure.'

She wrinkled her nose. 'Aye, right.'

'And to tell Colin he's sorry . . . sorry for what?'

'Sorry he killed him.' She started walking down the corridor, trying hard not to limp. 'He thinks he killed his brother.'

'But Colin must have visited?'

'A few times, yes.'

'Only a few?'

She stopped again, turned to face him. 'How would you feel if every time your brother saw you he thought you were a ghost?'

Rebus could think of no reply, so gave a shrug. Satisfied with this, she went a few more paces, then stopped at a swing door, ready with her palm against its surface.

'Thanks for your help,' she said.

'My name's John.'

She nodded at this information. 'You're a friend of Mr Flatley. Did he tell you his theory?'

'He thinks people are dying.'

'And what do you think, John?'

'I think you get lousy pay for back-breaking work.'

'And?' Her face was almost breaking into a smile.

'And you do the best you can for your patrons.'

She nodded slowly, pushed open the door and disappeared through it into what seemed to be the kitchen.

*   *   *

The painting had been removed from the entrance hall. There was no sign of either Ken Flatley or Donald Morrison. Outside, Morrison's Merc had gone from the car park. As Rebus manoeuvred his own rusting Saab down the driveway, slowing for the speed bumps, each one a potential nail in his car's coffin, he had to pull on to the verge so a delivery van could pass him His eyes sought the driver's, expecting some gesture of thanks at the show of courtesy, but the man stared resolutely ahead. The side of the white transit bore the legend 'Pakenham Fresh Fleshing'. Rebus stayed on the verge and watched in his rearview as the van rattled towards its destination. He knew the driver from somewhere; seemed to recognise the face. It was the jaw-line, the set of the mouth. Maybe from a butcher's shop, but he didn't know the name Pakenham. All the same, he was reminded that he needed something for dinner. Steak pie maybe, and a tin of marrowfat peas. Or he could always eat out, provided he could find a dinner partner. He thought again of Annie and those deep hazel eyes. Shame she wore a wedding ring. His mobile started ringing. He fished it out of his pocket and checked the display, then held it to his ear.

'How do you fancy dinner tonight,

my treat?'

'And will there be any solids involved?' a voice replied.

'Some,' he promised, knowing that Detective Sergeant Siobhan Clarke had already taken the bait.

*   *   *

Diners in the Oxford Bar needed no menu. There was the Cambridge Bar further along Young Street if you really wanted a meal. The Ox, on the other hand, served pies and bridles (until they ran out), and filled rolls—corned beef and beetroot a speciality. Snacks consisted of crisps, nuts and pork scratchings.

'Yummy,' Siobhan Clarke said.

'We can hit a chip shop later if you're not replete,' Rebus responded, placing her vodka and lemonade on the table. She'd settled for a ham and tomato roll. The barman had gone to some lengths to also supply a crusty jar of French mustard. Rebus pulled out a chair and settled himself. Two inches were already missing from his pint of IPA. A macaroni cheese pie sat on the plate before him. 'It was the last hot thing they had,' he explained now.

'I can imagine.'

He took a bite and shrugged. Siobhan spread mustard thinly across the roll, and closed it up again. 'How was Ken?' she asked, lifting the roll to her mouth.

'He says the inmates are dropping like flies—his exact words.'

'Meaning?'

'Meaning a few of his fellow codgers have caught the last train.'

'Isn't that what happens when you get old?'

Rebus nodded his agreement. 'Something else happened while I was out there.'

She ate in silence as Rebus told her the story of Lionel Waters. By the end of it, he'd finished his first pint. He raised the empty glass. She

28

shook her head, letting him know she didn't yet need a refill.

'I mean it's your shout,' he said.

When she made to get up, he beat her to it. 'Only kidding: you're my guest, remember?'

By the time he returned from the bar, she had finished her roll and was swirling the ice cubes in what was left of her drink.

'I bought my car from Waters Motors,' she told him.

'So did half the city.'

'I'd never heard about a brother, though.'

'Me neither.'

'He's lucky he wasn't lobotomised —they used to do that, you know.'

'You mean they don't any more?'

She saw that he was teasing. 'John F. Kennedy's sister . . . I was reading about her only the other day.'

'He had a sister?'

'She died recently. Locked up for sixty years . . .'

'And given a lobotomy?'

'That's right.'

'Well, we don't do that any more.'

They sat in silence for a moment, concentrating on their drinks. Siobhan was first to speak. 'What is it?' she asked.

'How do you mean?'

'Something's bugging you. I hope it's not gold fever.'

'What are you talking about?'

'Tales of hidden treasure.' She widened her eyes theatrically. 'They've sent many a man mad before you.'

'Sod off, Siobhan.'

She laughed. 'But there *is* something, isn't there?'

'It's what he said when he was standing in front of me.'

'What?'

'"I'm not what you think I am". He said "what" rather than "who".'

Siobhan snapped her fingers 'They've swapped places! Lionel is Colin and vice versa—that's how it would work in a film.'

'I'm warning you . . . ' Rebus stared into his beer. 'And he said "she"— "she buried the body". He wanted to say sorry to his brother.'

Siobhan leaned across the table. 'We're not psychiatrists, John.'

'I know that.'

'We're *detectives*.'

'That's right.' He looked up at her. 'You're absolutely right.'

His tone alerted her. She sat back again, hands resting around her empty glass. 'What are you going to do?'

'For now, I'm going to get you a refill.' He pushed himself to his feet.

'And after?'

'You said it yourself, Shiv: I'm a detective.'

'You're going to see the car man, aren't you?'

A smile flitted across Rebus's face. 'If nothing else, maybe he'll do me a trade-in on the Saab . . .'

*   *   *

The main Edinburgh showroom for Waters Motors was just off Calder Road. Rebus headed there next morning, the rush-hour traffic numbing his senses, so that he happily accepted the secretary's offer of caffeine.

'Instant okay?' she'd asked apologetically.

'Instant's fine.' Colin Waters had yet to arrive from his home in Linlithgow, but that didn't bother Rebus. He had a call to make: to the Scottish Criminal Records Office. During part of the crawl here, he'd stared at the blacked-out windows of the van in front, and this had triggered a memory—a name, which in turn had brought another name into play. He gave both to his SCRO colleague, along with his mobile phone number.

'How soon till you call me?' he asked. He was seated on the showroom's mezzanine level, its

32

smoked-glass walls giving a view of the business area below. The cars on display gleamed. Their very tyres sparkled, picked out by well-positioned halogen bulbs suspended from the ceiling. The salesmen were young and wore commission-bought suits, which made it easy to spot the most successful ones. When the revolving door spat out a newcomer, those who had been sitting leaped to their feet, eyes seeking an acknowledgement from the elderly man in the sagging jacket and slacks.

Colin Waters.

He was in his seventies, much the same age as his brother, but there the similarity ended. Colin Waters was about a foot shorter than Lionel, and boasted a thick head of hair and a face grown pink and round from indulgence. Ignoring the greetings from those around him, he started climbing the open-sided glass staircase, a busy man with a crowded schedule ahead. He glanced at Rebus as he passed him, perhaps mistaking him for a rep of some kind. He closed the office door after him, and Rebus thought he could hear the muffled conversation that followed. When the door opened again, Colin Waters gestured with a crooking of his finger. Rebus thought about staying put—just to see how the man would react—but decided against it. He followed Waters into the office, accepted the mug from the secretary, and watched her leave, closing the door quietly behind her.

There were two desks: one for the secretary, one for her boss. Rebus decided that the proximity had to be for one of two reasons: either Waters liked looking at her, or else he didn't want to miss anything going on around him. Waters was gesturing again, this time for Rebus to sit, but Rebus stayed standing. There was a full-height glass wall here, again looking down on to the sales floor.

Rebus pretended to be watching from it, mug cupped in front of him.

'Elaine says you're a police officer,' Waters barked, landing heavily on his own leather-upholstered chair and pulling it in towards his desk.

'That's right, sir. CID.'

'You wouldn't tell her what it's about. All very mysterious.'

'Not really, sir. Just didn't think you'd want me discussing family matters in front of the staff.' When Rebus turned his head, the blood was draining from Waters' face.

'Lionel?' he gasped.

'Don't worry, sir, your brother's fine.' Rebus decided finally to sit down.

'Then what's . . . not Martha?'

'Martha?'

'My sister.' Waters caught himself. 'Obviously not, since you don't know who I'm talking about.'

Rebus was remembering Lionel's words: *she buried the body.* 'Actually, sir, it is about your brother. I happened to be at Renshaw House yesterday, and had to help the staff restrain him. Seems he wanted to walk out of there, so he could find you and say sorry.'

'Oh Christ.' Waters bowed his head, pinching the skin at the bridge of his nose.

'You know he thinks he killed you?'

Colin Waters nodded. 'Right from when he was a kid, we knew there was something that wasn't right about him. He was a lot of fun, though . . . boisterous, you know?' He seemed to expect some response, so Rebus produced a slow nod. 'But he never seemed to have any sense of when he was taking things too far. He'd bite . . . lash out . . . even at strangers on the street. Our parents decided he needed to be kept home, at least for as long as they were able.' He took a deep breath. 'Martha and I . . . we tried to pretend he was just like anybody else.' He broke off, flicked at something invisible on the arm of his jacket. 'Special needs is the term these days: back then, the local children had other ways of putting it. Keeping Lionel at home became problematic.'

'It couldn't have been easy,' Rebus acknowledged. Waters gave the briefest of smiles.

'We were wrestling one day,' he said. 'Middle of July —teenagers, the pair of us—out on the lawn. Lionel loved to wrestle . . . probably fell on me a bit too solidly—he was well-built in those days.'

'What happened?'

'I think I passed out. When I came to, he was up to high doh . . . reckoned he'd done me in. We couldn't make him see sense.'

'By "we" you mean . . .?'

'Martha and me. She's younger than us. The way he was carrying on, it scared the hell out of her—roaring like a wild beast, almost foaming at the mouth. As far as Lionel was concerned, I was a ghost . . .'

Waters paused, lost in memory. His fingers had stretched out to touch a photo frame on his desk. Rebus could see only the back of it.

'Is that . . .?' He pointed to the frame.

'This is afterwards. Me and Martha.'

'Do you mind if I take a look?'

Waters' shoulder twitched as he turned the photo round. It was black and white, and showed Colin Waters still not quite out of his teens. His sister looked four or five years younger, breasts just beginning to appear, hair still held in pigtails. They were seated on the staircase of what appeared to be a grand house— probably not dissimilar to Renshaw House. They were peering through the iron banisters. There was a painting on the wall behind them. Neither looked particularly happy, and the photographer had failed to get their faces in sharp focus. There was a ghostly quality to the whole. Rebus couldn't help wondering why the photo was so important. To him, it seemed a daily reminder of something lost: the hopes and dreams of youth.

'Interesting painting,' he said, as Waters turned the photo back towards himself.

'It's still in the family'

'Is it a loch or a river?'

'I think the artist invented it, whatever it is. Not too many clifftop castles in Scotland.'

'Not that I know of.' Rebus made to rise to his feet, Waters following suit.

'I'm still not sure why you came, Inspector,' he commented.

'Me neither,' Rebus told him. Then he slid his hands into his pockets. 'Your brother just seemed so confused and lonely. I take it a visit from you would upset him?'

Waters shrugged. 'I'm a ghost, remember.'

'And your sister? Does she see him much?'

Waters shook his head. 'It upsets her too much to see him like that.' He gestured with an expansive right arm. 'Now, if there's nothing else . . . '

'I appreciate your time, sir.' Rebus didn't bother mentioning the Saab; reckoned it would do him another year.

*   *   *

He decided that a further visit to Renshaw House was in order, but first drove towards his home in Marchmont, stopping at the local butcher's shop. He was a known face here, and as with a good barman, the butcher knew what his regulars liked.

'Steak pie, Mr Rebus?' he was asking as Rebus walked over the threshold.

'No thanks, Andy.'

'Couple of nice pork chops then.'

Rebus shook his head. There was sawdust on the floor—for show rather than anything else. Andy wore a striped apron and straw boater. Photos on the white-tiled wall showed his father in the selfsame get-up. Rebus was struck again by what the photo on Waters' desk must have meant to the car dealer.

'Just a question actually, Andy,' he said.

'Is this me becoming a police informer? The Huggy Bear of Edinburgh?'

Rebus answered the laugh with a smile of his own. He'd never seen the butcher at rest. Even now, with no order to fill, Andy was sorting the display of various hams and sausages. 'I was wondering if you knew about a butcher called Pakenham.'

'Pakenham?'

Rebus spelled it for him 'They'd be local, I think "Fresh Fleshing" is what it says on their van.'

'Have they got a shop?'

'I've only seen the van. It was delivering to an old folk's home.' Andy pursed his lips.

'What is it?' Rebus asked.

'Well, it's not always top-grade, is it?'

'Cheap cuts, you mean?'

'Cheapest possible.' Andy held his hands up. 'I'm not saying they're all like that . . .'

'But some are?' Rebus nodded to himself. 'Got a phonebook, Andy?'

The butcher fetched one from the back of the shop. Rebus checked, but there was no Pakenham Fresh Fleshing.

'Thanks, Andy,' he said, handing it back.

'Sorry I can't be more help. More Yogi Bear than Huggy, eh?'

'Actually, you've been a big help. And maybe I will take one of those steak pies.'

'Family size, as usual?'

'As usual, Andy,' Rebus

confirmed. He would drop it home before his visit to Renshaw House.

*   *   *

He rang the bell and waited. It was late afternoon now, the sun low in the sky. The detached villa sat on Minto Street, a busy thoroughfare on the city's south side. The house had a faded elegance to it, its stonework blackened by time and traffic. Most of the houses around it had become bed and breakfasts, but not this one. The name on the unpolished brass door-plate was Waters, the letters picked out in verdigris. The sister, it seemed, had never married.

She opened the door herself. No pigtails now, the hair grey and thin, scraped back from the forehead and tucked behind both ears. Her eyes were sunken, as were her cheeks. Colin Waters, it seemed, had stolen all the heartiest genes from his parents.

'Martha Waters?' Rebus said, realising that he was pitching his voice a little louder than was probably necessary—she was probably only ten years older than him.

'Yes?'

He held open his warrant card. 'I'm from the police, Miss Waters. Do you mind if I come in?'

She said nothing, her mouth forming a crumpled O. But she held the door open so he could pass into the hall. It wasn't the same one as in the photograph. The banisters were wooden, darkly varnished. The only natural light came from a window on the upstairs landing. The carpet was ornate but as worn as its owner. She closed the door, adding to the pervasive gloom. Rebus noted an alarm panel on the wall beside the umbrella stand. The panel looked new, with a digital display. A sensor blinked in the far corner of the ceiling.

'Would you care for a cup of tea?' She spoke quietly, pronouncing each syllable. She had yet to ask him why he was here.

'Is there somewhere we can sit, Miss Waters?'

She shuffled in her carpet-slippers towards another door, opening it to reveal what she would probably call the parlour. It was like stepping back in time: antimacassars on the sofas, an empty three-tiered cake-stand on a large embroidered doily. Little ornaments and knick-knacks covered every surface. A grandfather clock had ceased to work some time back, frozen for ever at one minute to twelve.

'Did you say you wanted tea?' she enquired.

'No thanks.' Rebus had strode over to the fireplace, admiring the large painting framed above the mantel. A bus sped past outside, causing some of the ornaments to rattle. Martha Waters sat herself down. Before his arrival, she'd been listening to the radio: a classical station, the sound barely audible. Nothing much wrong with her hearing then . . . or she was just saving batteries.

'This is a grand painting,' Rebus told her.

'I used to like it,' she said 'I hardly see it any more.'

Rebus nodded his understanding. Nothing wrong with her eyes either; she meant something else entirely.

Who's it by?' he asked.

'My brother says it's a Gainsborough.'

'Explains the alarm system . . . I take it Colin had it fitted?'

'Do you know about art?'

Rebus shook his head. 'But I know the name. It must be quite old then.'

'Seventeen-eighties.'

'As old as that? And worth a bit, I dare say?'

'Six figures, so Colin tells me.'

Rebus shook his head again, this time in apparent wonder. 'I saw that photograph of it. You know the one I mean?' He turned to her. 'Colin keeps it on his office desk. It stares back at him every working day.'

Her eyes seemed to regain their focus. 'What is it you want here?'

'Me?' He shrugged. 'I just wanted to see it in the flesh. I thought maybe you'd've sold it or something.'

'We could never sell it.'

'Not even after what you went through to get it?'

'I don't know what you mean.'

'I think you do, Miss Waters. I think it's been your little secret all these long years. I've just come from Renshaw House, had a nice long chat with Lionel.'

At mention of her brother's name, Martha stiffened, clasping her hands on her lap in front of her.

'All those crazy stories he tells . . . about his treasure and how he killed his brother . . . and how *you* buried him. He keeps rambling about a boat and a castle.' Rebus pointed to the

47

painting. 'And there they are: a castle on a hilltop, fishing boat on the water below it—Lionel's treasure. My bet is, he loved that painting and your parents had decided he could have it. Maybe they were going to will it to him, I don't know. But Colin wanted it, didn't he? And you, young as you were, you wanted it too. Two greedy little kids.' Rebus was standing in front of her now. He crouched so that she couldn't escape his eyes. 'Two brothers having a wrestle. Colin told me Lionel loved to wrestle, but Lionel says he never did: the wrestling was Colin's idea.' Rebus paused for effect. 'And then one of them's not moving, and he's covered in blood. What was it, Martha— ketchup? Paint? Whatever it was, it did the trick, sent Lionel over the edge. Especially when you told him *you'd* buried Colin.' Rebus stayed in a crouch, but her eyes had drifted to the painting.

'We could never sell it, not after

that. We never meant—' She broke off, took a deep breath. 'We didn't stop to think.'

'You were just a girl, Martha. How were you supposed to know it wasn't a game, some sort of joke? But Colin was that bit older than you . . . old enough to know exactly what he was doing. More than half a century Lionel's been kept shut up.'

'It would have happened anyway,' she said in a whisper, a tear trickling from one eye. 'We couldn't have coped. He was driving our parents demented . . . nice as ninepence one minute, flying off the handle the next. Schizophrenic, the doctors said. He was turning us into pariahs.'

'You mean the local kids called him names?'

'Not just Lionel . . . all of us. We were "the weird ones", the "loonies".' She wiped a hand across her face. 'Do you know how much he's cost us? All the family money, soaked up by care for Lionel.'

'Soaked up by guilt, if you ask me. That's why neither of you could let the painting go.' He rose to his feet. 'All these years . . . ' He let the words hang in the dusty air. His whole body felt dried out by this house, as if the life were being drained from him.

'What will happen to us?' she asked, her voice trembling.

'Lionel's not going to be in that home much longer—nobody is. So you'll offer him a room here, with his painting above his bed. And if you die before him, you'll make sure the painting goes to him.'

She looked up. 'That's all?'

Rebus offered a shrug. 'Anything you've just told me, Colin will deny—he's got too much to lose. I'd be delighted to see the pair of you in court, but I can't see that happening. I could dig into your parents' wills, any changes in them, see if the painting was to be Lionel's at any stage, but I'm not sure I'd get anywhere. So . . . yes, Miss Waters, that's all.' He started to walk towards the door, but paused.

'You *could* own up, of course, tell Lionel what the two of you did. But I wouldn't, if I were you. It might be too much for him. So don't think of letting Colin near him . . . and pray Lionel stays in good health, because if I hear otherwise . . . well, I might have to do that digging after all.'

*   *   *

The Suruchi restaurant was Rebus's idea—and his treat.

'Felt I short-changed you last night,' he'd explained to Siobhan.

After ordering their starters and main courses, they snapped off pieces of poppadom from a central shared plate, dipping them in chutney and biting down on them.

And Rebus told his story.

'Amazing,' she said as he finished. He was drinking lager for a change, while she stuck to mineral water.

'But you're not going to explain it all to Lionel?'

'Even if I got through to him, would it change anything?'

'His whole life's been . . . ' She couldn't quite find the right words.

'How does that old song go? "If I could turn back time . . . " If I could, believe me, I would.'

'It would be handy,' she conceded. 'We'd solve the crimes before they were ever committed.'

'Didn't do Tom Cruise much good in that film.' Their waiter had appeared at the table to clear away the empty plate. Siobhan brushed crumbs from her lap. 'Something else I did today,' Rebus was adding.

'What?'

'Solved Ken Flatley's little mystery.'

She looked at him. 'Who's been a busy boy then?'

He shrugged. 'Easy enough once I'd remembered the face driving the meat van. Belongs to a guy called

Bernie Cable. I arrested him once at Ingliston Market.'

'A Trading Standards bust?'

Rebus nodded. 'Cable was selling dodgy meat from a van.'

'Is this something I should be hearing prior to dinner?'

'Chicken breasts past their sell-by . . . that sort of stuff.'

'And now he's selling meat to care homes?'

'Until today he was. I've been on to Environmental Health . . . the council . . . Trading Standards.'

'You *have* been busy.'

'That's not the half of it. When I asked the Records Office to look up Cable, I gave them Donald Morrison's name too.'

'That suspicious mind of yours.' Siobhan leaned back as a clean plate was placed before her. Another waiter stood ready with orders of pakora and kebab.

'It was the way Morrison addressed me,' Rebus explained. 'He kept calling me "Inspector", even though I'd made it clear I wasn't there in any official capacity.'

'And that got your antennae clicking?'

'Made me think I might not be the first cop he'd ever had dealings with.'

'And?'

'And his name's not really Morrison—that's one of his many aliases. Real name's Charles Kirkup. He's been done for fraud.'

'You reckon he was in cahoots with Cable?'

'I contacted the hospital about those poor old sods who died. Food poisoning didn't show up on the original autopsies, but they're going to check again. It's like Ken said: the pathologists aren't always so rigorous when the corpse was on its last legs anyway.'

'So he was right, after a fashion?'

Rebus nodded.

'And you've told the council this?' Another nod. 'So now he'll be closed down?'

'Bound to be.'

'And where will Ken go?'

'I told him you had a spare room.' Rebus bit into a kebab.

'I've got a better idea,' Siobhan said, spooning sauce over her pakora. 'Colin Waters will know an investment when he sees one. He could keep the place open, maybe just promote one of the staff to manage it.'

Rebus saw those hazel eyes again. 'And why would he do that?'

'You could tell him there's a Gainsborough resting on it,' Siobhan said coyly. 'And after all, if he owns Renshaw House, he won't have to pay for Lionel's care any more. I'm sure you could get Martha to argue your case for you.'

Rebus was thoughtful. 'Maybe I could at that.'

'Atonement, I think it's called.'

'Whatever it's called, I'll drink to it,' Rebus said, raising his glass.